THE ANIMAL BOOGIE

THE ANIMAL BOOGIE

Debbie Harter

SCHOLASTIC INC.
New York Toronto London Auckland Sydney
Mexico City New Delhi Hong Kong

Down in the jungle, come if you dare!
What can you see shaking here and there?
With a shaky shake here and a shaky shake there,
What's that creature shaking here and there?

IT'S A BEAR!
She goes shake, shake, boogie, woogie, oogie!
Shake, shake, boogie, woogie, oogie!
Shake, shake, boogie, woogie, oogie!
That's the way she's shaking here and there.

Down in the jungle where nobody sees,
What can you see swinging through the trees?
With a swingy swing here and a swingy swing there,
What's that creature swinging through the trees?

IT'S A MONKEY!
He goes swing, swing, boogie, woogie, oogie!
Swing, swing, boogie, woogie, oogie!
Swing, swing, boogie, woogie, oogie!
That's the way he's swinging through the trees.

Down in the jungle in the midday heat,
What can you see stomping its feet?
With a stompy stomp here and a stompy stomp there,
What's that creature stomping its feet?

IT'S AN ELEPHANT!
She goes stomp, stomp, boogie, woogie, oogie!
Stomp, stomp, boogie, woogie, oogie!
Stomp, stomp, boogie, woogie, oogie!
That's the way she's stomping her feet.

Down in the jungle where the trees grow high,
What can you see flying in the sky?
With a flappy flap here and a flappy flap there,
What's that creature flying in the sky?

IT'S A VULTURE!
He goes flap, flap, boogie, woogie, oogie!
Flap, flap, boogie, woogie, oogie,
Flap, flap, boogie, woogie, oogie!
That's the way he's flying in the sky.

Down in the jungle where the leaves lie deep,
What can you see learning how to leap?
With a leapy leap here and a leapy leap there,
What's that creature learning how to leap?

IT'S A LEOPARD!
She goes leap, leap, boogie, woogie, oogie!
Leap, leap, boogie, woogie, oogie!
Leap, leap, boogie, woogie, oogie!
That's the way she's learning how to leap.

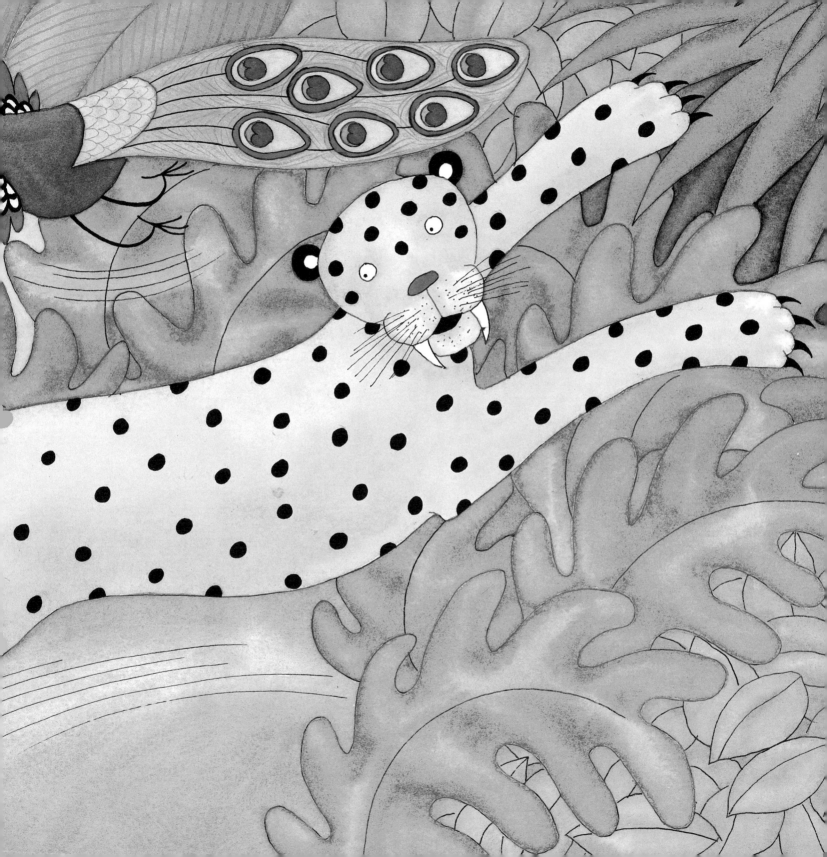

Down in the jungle where there's danger all around,
What can you see slithering on the ground?
With a slither slither here and a slither slither there,
What's that creature slithering on the ground?

IT'S A COBRA!
He goes slither, slither, boogie, woogie, oogie!
Slither, slither, boogie, woogie, oogie!
Slither, slither, boogie, woogie, oogie!
That's the way he's slithering on the ground!

Down in the jungle where the stars are shining bright,
Who can you see swaying left and right?
With a sway sway here and a sway sway there,
Who is swaying left and swaying right?

WE ARE!
We go sway, sway, boogie, woogie, oogie!
Sway, sway, boogie, woogie, oogie!
Sway, sway, boogie, woogie, oogie!
That's the way we boogie through the night!

let's stomp!

let's slither!

let's sway!

The Animal Boogie

ISBN 0-439-26504-5

Text copyright © 2000 by Barefoot Books. Illustrations copyright © 2000 by Debbie Harter. All rights reserved. Published by Scholastic Inc., 555 Broadway, New York, NY 10012, by arrangement with Barefoot Books. SCHOLASTIC and associated logos are trademarks and/or registered trademarks of Scholastic Inc.

12 11 10 9 8 7 6 5 4 3 2 1   0 1 2 3 4 5/0

Printed in the U.S.A.   08

First Scholastic printing, December 2000

The moral right of Debbie Harter to be identified as the illustrator of this work has been asserted. This book was typeset in One Stroke Script Infant 26 on 30 point. The illustrations were prepared in watercolor, crayon, pen and ink on thick watercolor paper. Graphic design by Judy Linard, England.

For Tuppence and Aeron — D. H.
For Suzie and Freya with love — N. T.